GREED, FLESH, AND FANTASY

BY CODY GOODFELLOW

Long before we understood anything about how reality works, we were searching for the cheat codes.

Do a dance and sprinkle water to make it rain. Sacrifice an animal to the gods to secure a bountiful harvest. Humans always have and always will try to ritual games to shape the world around us, playing by secret rules intuited or handed down from higher powers from Outside, where the script of all creation is written. Demons, gods and reality itself must bend to the will of the wise sorcerer.

But what makes magic magic? Does it work because of our belief, because of the demons and angels waiting only for the magic words to be uttered and the right sacrifice?

If it is our belief, the energy invested in it that gives magic its power, then sex is our most powerful spells. "Sex is, directly or indirectly, the most powerful weapon in the armoury of the Magician," wrote Aleister Crowley in Magick Without Tears, "and precisely because there is no moral guide, it is indescribably dangerous." Like any magical discipline, the physical act of love—the little death, the communion of flesh—is itself a ritual, a sacrament, and a forbidden secret. Those adept in its arts can wreak havoc or spread harmony far beyond the domain of their own beds. Fame and mass-marketed sex appeal are chaos magic that as often as not spins out of control and destroys those rash enough to wield it.

Fantasy art abounds that caters to every erotic taste, but few illustrators have conjured more vividly the magical aspect of the carnal, or explored more fearlessly the unintended consequences of sex—than Mike Dubisch. In The Doula's Exile, he lets sumptuously alien forms tell their own stories of desire and strange fulfillment to embellish the spare confession of his script. Here, love itself is a mutating force that writes its fickle messages in flesh.

Need a shower yet? You will…

In The Corpse's Crusade, sorcerous perversions of greed and lust tests the tired barbarian trope to destruction, but the avid sexual energy animating even the deadest of his subjects only escalates until the orgiastic climax. Loosely inspired by Clark Ashton Smith's Zothique cycle of dark fantasy stories, it's the kind of thing we all wish Heavy Metal was still doing.

We will return to our regular programming next issue, but we hope you will look out for future reissues of Mike's incomparable sequential art with Weirdling, and The Crypt Kid.

FORBIDDEN FUTURES 9
WRITTEN BY CODY GOODFELLOW   ART BY MIKE DUBISCH
THE CORPSE'S CRUSADE
IN ALL OF ZOTHIQUE, NO IDOL OR MEMORIAL FANE STANDS TALLER THAN THE MONUMENT TO THRASCUS OF XYLAC, WHO NEVER SOUGHT GLORY.
THE SONGS OF HIS EXPLOITS ARE STILL SUNG IN THE RUINS OF MINARETTED AVANDRA, BUT FEW KNOW THE TRUTH...
THE CONQUEST THAT MADE A LEGEND OF THE MAN ONLY BEGAN WITH HIS DEATH.
NONE WERE BOLDER OR MORE RUTHLESS THAN THRASCUS, IF THE PRICE WAS RIGHT.
BUT KING VUKROTA COULD NOT OFFER HIM ENOUGH TO LEAD HIS RAIDERS INTO THE ZHEL HINTERLANDS TO PURGE THE FEARSOME GHORII.
TOO CRAVEN TO LEAD HIS OWN ARMY, TOO GREEDY TO PAY A FAIR WAGE...
YET KING VUKROTA WAS MORE THAN EQUAL TO THE TASK OF MURDER...
THUS WAS THE GREAT MERCENARY BOUGHT FOR A FISTFUL OF STEEL AND A SINGLE GOLD COIN.
THE SPIRIT OF THRASCUS WAS TOO WEAK FOR THE GEAS OF KING VUKROTA...
BUT UNDER THE MINISTRATIONS OF AVANDRA'S ROYAL MAGI, HIS FLESH SOON PROVED WILLING ENOUGH.

SO LONG AS THE ENCHANTED COIN EXISTED, THE DEAD MAN COULD NEVER REST...
AND ONLY ITS POSSESSOR COULD HOPE TO TURN HIM FROM HIS MISSION.
THE WIZARDS ENTRUSTED THE COIN TO THE KING, WHO NO DOUBT PUT IT IN A SAFE PLACE.
HIS SWORDSMEN AWOKE TO FIND THEIR MASTER ODDLY TACITURN...
BUT HE STILL LED THE WAY TO SLAUGHTER AND RICHES...
AND SO THEY FOLLOWED.
THROUGH YMORTH AND CITH THEY MARCHED, SLAYING ALL THEY MET ON THE ROAD.
SOON ENOUGH, THEY CAME TO THE HINTERLANDS OF ZHEL...
AND THE DOMAIN OF THE GHORII.
FOR ALL THEIR MIGHT, THE THRALLS OF THRASCUS COULD NOT SUBDUE THE GHORII HORDE.
INDEED, THEY BARELY SERVED TO SUBDUE THEIR HUNGER...
AS BATTLEFIELD BECAME BANQUET, THRASCUS STOOD ALONE...
TOO HEROIC-- OR TOO RANCID-- TO BE DEVOURED.

THE GHORII BROUGHT HIM BEFORE THEIR QUEEN, THE ENCHANTRESS QARIONA.
NO MORTAL MAN COULD RESIST HER...
BUT NONE COULD QUENCH HER NECROPHILOUS LUST...
WHICH COULD ONLY BE SATED BY THE RIGOR OF THE TOMB.

WITH FEMININE WILES AND BLACKEST SORCERY, QARIONA BENT THE EMPTY VESSEL OF THRASCUS TO HER LASCIVIOUS WILL.

WHEN HER DEBAUCHERIES OFFENDED EVEN THE CORPSE-EATING GHORII, HE REPELLED HER WOULD-BE USURPERS.
BY SLOW TURNS, AS ONLY A CORPSE COULD, HE WON HER HEART.

EAGER FOR ANY ADVANTAGE, THE GHORII MAGE WYRUXTOS SPIED UPON HIS LOVESICK QUEEN...
AND IN THE CARELESS MURMURING OF HER BEDCHAMBER, HE FOUND THE KEY.
INVOKING THE CHARNEL-GOD MORDIGGIAN, WYRUXTOS STOLE THE TRUE NAME OF QARIONA'S BELOVED...
AND WITH IT THE REINS OF HIS BLACK, UNBEATING HEART.

EVEN IN DEATH, THRASCUS WAS UNEQUALLED AT ANY TASK SET BEFORE HIM.
BUT NOW HE TOOK NO PLEASURE, NO PAYMENT.

HE HAD BECOME THE PERFECT MERCENARY...

BUT HIS NEW MASTERS PROVED AS FICKLE AS HIS OLD ONES, WHEN HIS WORK WAS DONE.

HIS USE AT AN END, THE GHORII CAST HIS BRAINLESS REMAINS...
INTO THE SUBTERRANEAN HEADWATERS OF THE MIGHTY RIVER VOUM.

WHEN HE FINALLY EMERGED FROM HIS RIVERINE SOJOURN, HE WAS RECOVERED BY SOME OTHERS...
COLDER THAN CADAVERS, YET THE DISCOVERY FILLED THEM WITH CLOCKWORK JOY.

LONG HAD THE AUTOMATONS OF DUIR SILUXIS SEARCHED FOR A VESSEL SUCH AS THIS ONE...

A STURDY HOST FOR THE UNBORN GODS THEY HAD MINED FROM THE DYING EMBERS OF THE INNER EARTH.

THE HUMBLE AUOMATA EXPECTED NO REWARD FOR THEIR SERVICE...
AND THEY RECEIVED NONE.

OUT INTO THE WIDE WORLD, THRASCUS OF XYLAC BORE THE BLACK HALO OF THE EMBRYONIC GODLINGS.
THE MEREST GLANCE AT HIS NAKED GLORY LEFT ALL IN HIS PATH BLIND AND RAVING MAD...
ALL WHO RESISTED HIS CALL TO WORSHIP WERE ENGULFED AND ADDED TO HIS MAJESTY.

CHAOS MAGICK
DID HE COME FOR REVENGE, TO COLLECT THE DEBT HE WAS OWED? OR TO BRING NEW FAITH TO THE DECADENT, GODLESS SONS OF MAN?
NONE CAN SAY WHY HE CAME... BUT RETURN HE DID TO AVANDRA...
AND THE PALACE OF KING VUKROTA!
ONLY WHEN BLINDED DID VUKROTA SEE THAT THE MERCENARY HE'D BOUGHT SO CHEAP HAD RETURNED TO CLAIM ALL HE HELD DEAR.
IF ONLY HE COULD RECALL WHERE HE PUT THE COIN...
WHILE THE BATTLE RAGED OUTSIDE, THE MAGI SEARCHED THE ROYAL TREASURY...
THEY COULD SENSE THE COIN'S CHARM, BUT ALL OF THEM WERE IDENTICAL.
THE KING ORDERED ALL OF THEM DESTROYED.
THEY TRIED IN VAIN TO DISENCHANT THE ABOMINATION...
BUT EVEN DREAD LORD THASAIDONDID NOT DEIGN TO INTERCEDE TO SAVE THEM.

NO ALTAR TO ANY GOD OF HUMANKIND EVER GROANED UNDER A GREATER TRIBUTE THAN THE COURT OF AVANDRA FED TO THE CAULDRON.
AND NO GOD WAS EVER LESS ATTENTIVE TO A PRAYER.

THUS ENDED THE REIGN OF KING VUKROTA...

THOUGH THE COURTIERS HAD FED EVERY OUNCE OF GOLD IN THE PALACE TO THE CAULDRON...
THEY ONLY FOUND THE ENCHANTED COIN JUST AS THRASCUS FOUND IT, HIMSELF.
IF KING VUKROTA'S FONDEST WISH WAS NEVER TO BE PARTED FROM HIS WEALTH, THEN TO BE ENCASED IN MOLTEN GOLD MUST'VE SEEMED LIKE HEAVEN.

FROZEN IN A SECOND, FINAL DEATH, THRASCUS HAD BECOME A GILDED TRAP FOR THE GOD-LARVAE...
BESET BY UNBELIEVERS, THEY WEAKENED AND EXPIRED... TAKING THE PROUD CAPITOL OF AVANDRA WITH THEM.

AND SO THE MORTAL HUSK OF THRASCUS OF XYLAC BECAME THE HEADSTONE OF THE CITY THAT USED HIM FOR THE PRICE OF A MEAL.
AND TRAVELLERS IN LATER AGES REMARKED THAT ANY CITY THAT SO HONORED ITS COMMON SOLDIERS...
MUST HAVE BEEN A BRAVE AND FAITHFUL ONE.

THE DOULA'S EXILE
BY MIKE DUBISCH

CHAOS MAGICK
I AM CAST OUT.
CAST OUT PHYSICALLY- AS I'VE ALWAYS BEEN OUTCAST.
NOW THE CURSE SO PLAINLY WRIT ACROSS MY FACE HAS, THEY SAY, COME BACK TO THEM.

PUNISHED THEY ARE, BY THE GODS FOR HAVING GRANTED ME THE ROLE OF MEDICINE WOMAN.
SHE WHOM NO MAN WOULD TOUCH.
ALLOWED THE PRIVILEGE OF PULLING INFANT CHILDREN AND GRANDCHILDREN FROM THE LOINS OF WIVES AND DAUGHTERS.
ONE LAST BURDEN.
TO CARRY MY DISGRACE OUT BEYOND THE VILLAGE WALLS.

WAAAAHH! WAHHAHA!
WAH! WAHA!

FORBIDDEN FUTURES 9

I BRING THE WAILING CHILD ALMOST TO THE EDGE OF THE VALLEY FLOOR BEFORE ABANDONING HIM TO THE WILD.
WAAAAHH!
WAAAAHH!
WAAAAHH!
WAAAAHH!

WAAAAHH! WAHHAHA!
WAH! WAHA!
WAH! WAH!
WAH! WAH!

FROM THERE I BEGIN MY ASCENT, AS CONDEMNED.
WAH! WAH!
WAH! WAH!
WAH! WAH!

THE PATH ELEVATES QUICKLY. PALE GREEN BLANKETS THE VALLEY BELOW.
I VOW TO CONTINUE MY ASCENT TILL DAWN.
I WOULD BE WELL CLEAR OF THE VILLAGE AND BE DRY-EYED ABOUT IT.
WAH! WAH! WAH! WAH! WAH! WAH!
IF CURSED I BE, THEN LET ME LEAVE IT BEHIND WITH THE CHILD'S WAILS.

I CLIMB AND TREK FOR A TIME, AND IT IS GOOD.
I KNOW THE NUTS AND BERRIES I CAN EAT...
AND SMALL GRUBS AND THINGS IF NEEDED, WHEN MY SUPPLY OF DRIED MEATS RUNS OUT.
I ENCOUNTER NO ONE, FOR THE VILLAGE IS FAR BELOW, AND NO ONE LIVES UP THE WALL.
CHAOS MAGICK
AHHHH! UNNNGH!
AHHHH!
UNNNGH!
AHHHH!

FORBIDDEN FUTURES 9
AHHHH!
UNNNGH!
AHHHH!
AHHHHH!
WAHHH!
WAAHHH!
20

WAHHH!
WAAHHH!
WAHHH!
WAAHHH!
CHAOS MAGICK
SHE MUST BE A PRINCESS
OF HER PEOPLE, OR ELSE
ALL THE PREGNANT ARE
TREATED AS SUCH.

I KNOW NOT THE SPEECH OF
THE PEOPLE OF THE CLIFFSIDE
DWELLINGS, BUT MY ARTS SERVE
THEM WELL AND I AM WELCOMED.

I DELIVER MANY OF THEIR FIERCE, ENORMOUS INFANTS.

JURISEH
-2007
/9

FORBIDDEN
FUTURES

DOWN IN THE VILLAGE OF THE VALLEY FLOOR I MID-WIFED COUNTLESS HEALTHY INFANTS, AND THEN SEVEN AFFLICTED CHILDREN, BEFORE I WAS EXILED.

THE PEOPLE OF THE CLIFFSIDE ARE FAR QUICKER IN JUDGEMENT.
DID THE CURSE REALLY ARRIVE WITH ME?
DOES THE CURSE WALK AWAY WITH ME?
CHAOS MAGICK

FORBIDDEN FUTURES 9
I AM DISTURBED BY MEMORIES OF THE MOUNTAIN GOAT HOOF, AS I CLIMB THE WALL.
IN THE VILLAGE, I MID-WIFED INFANTS CURSED WITH CHICKEN CLAW, CAT AND DOG PAW, SHEEP HOOF, AND PIG FOOT.
28

WOLF LEG. NOT ONE OF MINE, THIS BOY: TOO OLD. THE CURSE HAS BEEN IN THE VALLEY BEFORE.
CHAOS MAGICK

FORBIDDEN FUTURES 9

FORBIDDEN FUTURES 9
A FAREWELL HE DOESN'T UNDERSTAND,
ANY MORE THEN HE KNOWS THE
TABOOS WE HAVE BROKEN.

THE TOP OF THE WALL, THE LIP OF THE BOWL,
THE CREST OF THE VALLEY. THE INSECT MEN.

THEY PAY ME NO MIND AS THEY
CARRY THEIR BURDENS.

THEIR SHEER NUMBERS MAKE THE ACT I AM
OBSERVING SEEM BOTH RITUALISTIC AND
MECHANICALLY EFFICIENT.

I FOLLOW THE EMPTY-HANDED DRONES INTO THE HIVE.
IN THE QUEEN'S CHAMBER DRONES CONTINUE TO PULL STILLBORN GRUBS FROM HER MASSIVE WOMB. 
FORBIDDEN FUTURES 9

FORBIDDEN FUTURES 9

CHAOS MAGICK

FORBIDDEN FUTURES 9
THE QUEEN IS FAR DIFFERENT FROM THE PEOPLE OF THE VALLEY FLOOR OR THE CLIFFSIDE GIANTS... BUT MY ARTS SERVE HER WELL.
SHE ALLOWS ME TO STAY. AFTER A TIME MY WOMB SWELLS, TOO. THE BOY HAD LEFT ME A NEW BURDEN TO CARRY.

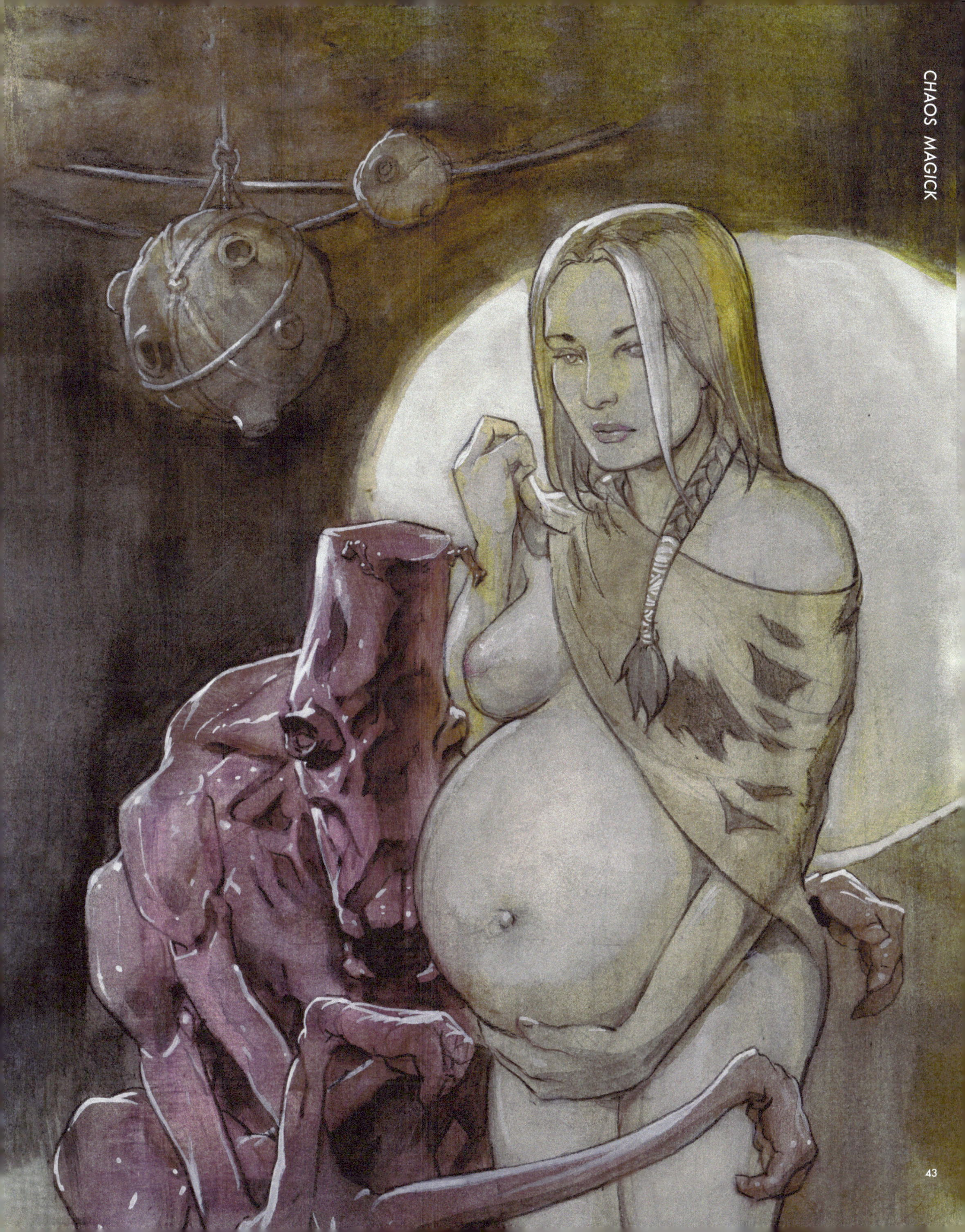

THE DRONES ACT ON MY INSTRUCTIONS.
FORBIDDEN FUTURES 9
THE BIRTHING
HOUR COMES
ON TIME.
44

FORBIDDEN FUTURES 9
THE INFANT STAYS WITH HIS PEOPLE. THEY WOULD KEEP HIM WELL.
MY EXILE CONTINUES, DOWN THE WALL, OVER THE CREST, AND BEYOND.

www.ingramcontent.com/pod-product-compliance
Lightning Source LLC
Chambersburg PA
CBHW041924180726
48295CB00002B/75